Nathan and the Knights:

Nathan Builds a Castle

By Kelly Epperson
Illustrated by Tashna Gill

To my kids. Dream big dreams,
and never give up. ~ K.E.

To my Mum, Jabeen. ~ T.G.

Once there was a brave young man named Nathan. Nathan lived on a farm with cows, chickens, pigs, goats, and his horses named Tig Tig and Roo Roo.

One day, Nathan rode Roo Roo out to check on the cows. He saw the great castle that the knights lived in. Nathan wanted to be a knight. Knights were brave and strong, and they kept the people safe. They always did what was right. Nathan looked up at the castle, and imagined what it would be like to be a knight.

2

That night he looked up at the moon and stars and prayed that one day he might become a knight.

The next day, Nathan got up very early to milk the cows. He put the milk jugs in his wagon and went to the market with Tig Tig and Roo Roo to sell the milk. When he got to the market, the castle was so close it seemed to stretch all the way to the sky. He saw knights standing on the castle wall in their shining, silver armor.

He was still staring at the knights when a man next to him yelled "Get out of my way! I'm busy. What are you staring at, anyway?"

"I was watching the knights," Nathan replied. "Do you know how I could become a knight?"

The man laughed and said, "You can't decide to be a knight! You have to be big and strong, and you have to be the son of a knight. If anybody could be a knight, do you think we would live out here? We would much rather live in the castle, but we can't be knights!" Nathan was surprised and sad to hear this. He liked his farm, but he really wanted to be a knight.

He said goodbye to the man, and went into the market. He didn't sell very much milk. He was sad about the bad news he had received and no one wanted to buy milk from a sad farmer.

Eventually he pretended to be happy, and people bought his milk. He felt better after selling the milk, but still felt sad about not being able to be a knight.

He rode home from the market disappointed. On the way home, he saw an old woman who had dropped a basket of eggs onto the soft grass. Some of them had rolled all the way to the bottom of the hill! He wanted to help, but it was getting dark and he knew that he still had to put his farm animals to bed. As he rode toward the old woman, he decided that the right thing to do was to help her, even if it seemed hard. "Would you like some help finding your eggs?" He asked. "Yes, please," she replied, so Nathan helped her find all of her eggs.

When Nathan had carried the last egg all the way to the top of the hill, he sat down on a rock and took off his hat to cool off. The old woman sat down beside him. "Thank you for helping me find my eggs," she said. "Now I will help you. Tell me why you are sad." Nathan told her about his dream of being a knight, and what the man had told him in the market. The old woman laughed. "That man is very silly. Of course I can tell you how to be a knight. Knights are brave, strong, and always do what is good. If you want to be a knight, all you have to do is be brave and strong, and always do what is good."

Nathan was confused, so he replied, "How will that make me a knight? That seems too simple and easy."

"Well, you are half right," the old woman replied, "It is simple but not easy. Every day, you must do a strong deed, a brave deed, and a good deed. Sometimes all three might be one deed, sometimes they might be different deeds."

"At the end of the day, you must decide if you have done all three deeds. If not, you must find ways to do them."

"If you cheat and convince yourself that something counts when you know it should not, then you will take even longer to become a knight, if you become one at all. If you do these deeds every day, then one day you will be a knight."

Nathan stared at the castle, then he said, "It sounds very hard, but I want to be a knight, so I will do all those deeds every day." The old woman smiled at him, and said, "You have already done a good deed today, by helping me. Now you need to do a strong and brave deed. Don't forget, these three deeds must be done every day."

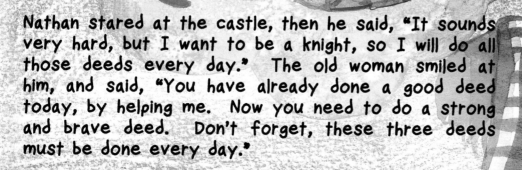

And with that, the old woman, her smile, and her eggs vanished. Nathan was very surprised, but it was getting dark. He was afraid of the dark woods, so he rushed to his wagon and hurried home. It was dark when he got there, but his animals were still out of the barn. He was afraid to go out in the dark, and he thought about leaving the animals out until the next morning. He wanted them to be safe, but he was afraid! Then he remembered that he still needed to do a brave deed. This was his chance! He gathered his courage, lit his lamp, and went out to face the darkness

Finding the animals took Nathan a long time, but eventually he put all of them in the barn and closed the door. He was very tired, and he headed to the house to go to sleep. He had just taken off his boots, when he remembered that he hadn't done anything strong that day!

He laced his boots up again, and went out into the dark. This time it did not seem as bad since he had been out all night anyway. He noticed that the water trough was nearly empty. He went to the well and raised the heavy jug from the bottom. He lifted it over his head and carried it to the trough.

After dumping it in, he wondered if lifting the jug had been enough, since it was heavy but not that heavy, and it had not been very hard to lift it just once. So he filled the jug and dumped it in the trough again and again, until he could not lift the jug any more.

Then he went back to his house, cleaned up, and went to sleep.

The next day he was on the lookout for brave, strong, and good deeds to do. He was on the lookout the next day, and the day after that. He did the three deeds every day. At first it was easy, but after a while, it seemed like deeds that were easy to find might be too easy to count, so he started looking for harder deeds to do. He got braver, stronger, and better at finding good deeds to do. As he grew, he looked for even harder things to do.

At first, his neighbors laughed at him, but when they saw how many good things he did for other people, they didn't laugh anymore. Instead, they all smiled whenever they saw Nathan.

Eventually, he was so brave, strong, and good at knowing the right thing to do that it was too easy to just do three things. He started doing every brave deed, strong deed, and good deed that he could find. He worked hard on his farm, and helped his neighbors with theirs. They admired him for being so brave, strong, and good. He told them to send him anyone who needed a brave, strong, or good deed done so that he could find enough deeds to do. Some days he was tired, but he knew that he would never be a knight if he missed even one day. Even on the days when he was tired, he made sure to do at least one brave, strong, and good deed.

Nathan continued his quest for many years, waiting to become a knight, and wondering how it would happen. The people who lived near the castle still laughed at him for thinking he could become a knight, but his neighbors trusted and looked up to him.

One day, a man from far away came to the little farm village, and told the people there was a great army coming. The army would burn their town and take their animals. When Nathan heard this, he stood up. Because everyone knew he was so brave, strong and good, they listened. "We have many days before the army will reach us," he said, "So we will ask for shelter in the castle, and we will take our animals there." The villagers thought this was a good idea, so they sent a messenger to the castle.

The messenger returned with bad news. "The castle does not have room for us," he said. When the people heard this, they were afraid, but Nathan stood up again. "If the castle and knights will not help us, we will have to help ourselves," he said, "We will be brave and strong, and we will build our own castle. It will be hard work, but if we all work together, we can save ourselves and our animals." The people felt a little better, but the work sounded hard, and they were still afraid.

With Nathan encouraging them and working with them, they started building. They dug rocks out of a quarry, shaped them into blocks, and mixed mortar. Then they stacked the blocks on top of each other and spread the mortar to hold the blocks together.

Then they built machines to build the high walls and also built houses inside the castle.

They also built a blacksmith shop so they could repair their tools. Lastly, they collected enough food to last for all the people and animals while they lived inside the castle.

When they were finally done, they moved their families and animals inside the castle. Everyone cheered for Nathan, and they celebrated their new castle with a great feast. .

Soon, the large army surrounded the castle, and demanded that the people give them all the money and animals or they would destroy the castle. Nathan told the people that they had nothing to worry about. They had food in the castle, and eventually the army would get hungry and leave.

The army was so big that even Nathan was afraid, but he had done brave deeds every day for so long that he knew being brave was the right thing to do. So Nathan stood strong on the castle wall where the whole army could see him and yelled down to them, "We will not surrender!"

The leaders of the army saw how brave he was, and were afraid to attack the castle. They decided to wait for the castle to run out of food.

The army waited and waited. Eventually, there was nothing left in the country for the army to eat. The army packed up and left the castle. The people rejoiced! Nathan had saved them all!

The villagers carried Nathan on their shoulders, and gave him a shield that the blacksmith had made for him. The villagers cheered for him. They all shouted together, "All hail Sir Nathan, knight of the castle!" Then Nathan saw the magical old woman waiting behind the crowd.

When the crowd left, Nathan followed the old woman to the top of the castle wall. As they reached the top, the old woman said, "You have done very well, but you are not done yet. Next you must convince the other knights that you are a knight, and then you will have to convince yourself. Convincing yourself is always the hardest. The only way to do that is to keep doing the three deeds every day. Good luck Nathan. Always do what is good." And with that, the old woman, her smile, and her wink vanished.

The End of the Beginning...

When I began this book, I wanted to write something my son would enjoy and also learn from. With hard work, we can all live our dreams. I want my kids to learn to dream big dreams, make plans to reach them, and work hard to achieve them. Perseverance and vision are powerful things.

I ask my kids questions as we read to make books more interactive. Here is one example question we might talk about for each page. Have fun making your own questions and dreaming big!

• How many of each animal are there?
• How many cows can you find?
• A constellation is a group of stars that make a picture. How many constellations do you see?
• How many flags do you see?
• What do you want to be when you grow up? How can you learn how to do that?
• Can you decide to be happy?
• How many eggs can you find?
• Are knights the only people who need to be brave, strong and good?
• Can you do these deeds every day?
• What brave deeds can you think of? Can you be brave for other people?
• How many fireflies can you see in the window? What strong deed did you do today?
• What are some strong deeds you can do?
• What are some good deeds that you can do?
• Does it matter if other people think you can't do something?
• Who can you ask for help when you need it?
• Why do you think Nathan was the only one brave enough to say anything?
• Is a big job easier to do by yourself, or with friends?
• Does it matter if some people laugh at you?
• Is it brave to stand up to someone who is doing the wrong thing?
• Is it brave to stand up for someone when they are being bullied?
• Do you remember what three deeds Nathan had to do every day?
• Can you remember to do a brave deed, a strong deed, and a good deed every day? Have you done these three deeds today?